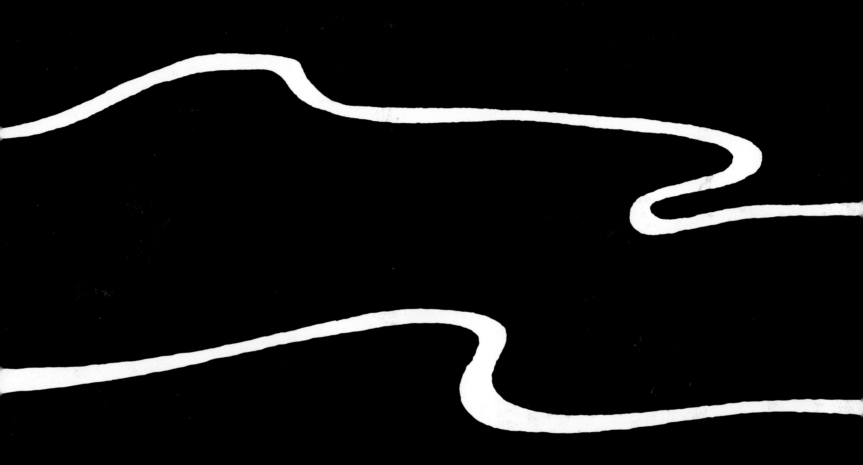

To little ghouls
everywhere,
especially
Finbar and Sally

Copyright © 1993 by Colin and Jacqui Hawkins

All rights reserved
First U.S. edition 1993
Published in Great Britain in 1993 by Walker Books Ltd., London.

Library of Congress Cataloging-in-Publication Data is available.

Library of Congress Catalog Card Number 92-54959

ISBN 1-56402-236-6
10 9 8 7 6 5 4 3 2 1

Printed in Singapore

The pictures in this book were done in pen, colored inks, and watercolors.

Come for a Ride on the
GHOST TRAIN

Colin & Jacqui
Hawkins

CANDLEWICK PRESS
CAMBRIDGE, MASSACHUSETTS

Come for a ride

on the Ghost Train.

In the dark, dark

Out in the slimy

forest you will ...

HHOWWL!

In the gruesom